Fanny
Saved the Day

Nalini Raghunandan

Illustrated by Frances Espanol

To order additional copies of this book, contact:
Xlibris
1-888-795-4274
www.Xlibris.com
Orders@Xlibris.com

Dedicated

To Kennedy—may your life be filled with beautiful stories.

It was a beautiful summer's day; the sun was shining brightly and there were a few white fluffy clouds in the sky.

The villagers filled the air with laughter and excitement as they made their way to the annual summer fair.

"It's time to go to the fair Fanny!" said Mr. Ed. It thrilled Fanny! He howled "AOOOOO!" Fanny walked ahead of the family, stopping along the way to greet the villagers and sniff the flowers.

Fanny spotted his new friend Pepita. They greeted each other playfully running and barking cheerfully. They also played fetch with a few kids.

Pepita is a dark grey schnauzer with a few spots of silver. Pepita and Fanny first met when Mr. Chuck took her for a walk by the seashore one morning. From that day onward, Fanny and Pepita were best friends.

The aroma of many delicious foods filled the air. There were many yummy treats, such as cotton candy, a variety of cookies, decorated cup cakes, ice-cream and snow cones. There were also many healthy rice, fish, and meat dishes.

The children were everywhere, having lots of fun at the many attractions and on the many rides.

There were horses, ponies and other farm animals, and a carriage ride for the children. The carriage was painted bright yellow, blue and red, and beautifully decorated with balloons and ribbons.

A few children—along with Fanny and Pepita—hopped into the carriage for a ride. They sang and giggled along the way, while Fanny and Pepita barked cheerfully.

The coachman stopped the carriage so the children could watch a juggler perform.

He twirled two lit fire sticks while he danced to music, and spun the sticks above his head like the top of a helicopter! The children cheered.

The juggler suddenly lost control of one stick and it flew out of his hand, landing right in the carriage. Oh, no!

The children screamed with fright. Wasting no time, Fanny leaped across the carriage and grabbed the flaming stick in his jaws.

He bounded towards the open field and dropped the stick a safe distance away. The villagers ran to Fanny and threw buckets of sand on the stick to put out the fire.

Mr. Ed and many villagers ran to the carriage to check on the children. Thankfully, the children were not hurt.

The children surrounded Fanny and took turns petting him. The juggler apologized to the children and the villagers and thanked Fanny with a big hug.

"Good boy! I am so sorry." He said.

Ms. Nazima—who owns a Pet Store and whose daughter was in the carriage—declared that Fanny could stop by for treats anytime.

The Village Mayor—dressed in her costume to perform in a culture dance—remembered Fanny's bravery at the seashore once before. She greeted Fanny and thanked him again for his quick thinking and heroism.

There was an award ceremony day for various competitions. The villager gave Fanny a medal for his selfless act that got the children out of harm's way. The inscription on the medal read: BRAVE DOG who saved the day.

CPSIA information can be obtained
at www.ICGtesting.com
Printed in the USA
BVHW021155141119
563829BV00002B/15/P